# THE
# HOUSE RABBIT

*For Robyn and Nic*

THE HOUSE RABBIT
A DAVID FICKLING BOOK
978 0 857 56018 6

Published in Great Britain by David Fickling Books,
a division of Random House Children's Books
A Random House Group Company

This edition published 2013

1 3 5 7 9 10 8 6 4 2

DAVID FICKLING BOOKS, 31 Beaumont Street, Oxford, OX1 2NP

www.kidsatrandomhouse.co.uk   www.totallyrandombooks.co.uk   www.randomhouse.co.uk

Addresses for companies within The Random House Group Limited can be found at:
www.randomhouse.co.uk/offices.htm

THE RANDOM HOUSE GROUP Limited Reg. No. 954009

A CIP catalogue record for this book is available from the British Library.

Printed and bound in China

# THE
# HOUSE RABBIT

Lesley White

David Fickling Books

In a dark, old house upon a hill, there
lived a well-trained House Rabbit.

One moonlit
night, Rabbit
woke with a start
and thought,
"What if the
house falls
down?"

At that very
moment there
was a terrible . . .

Poor Rabbit leapt up in a panic. He ran out of the bedroom and into the study.

"Why are you running so fast?" said Mouse, as Rabbit sent feathers flying.

"Come with me, the house is falling down!" Rabbit cried.

Mouse needed no more convincing and streaked after him.

They ran down the corridor and into the kitchen.

"Why are you running so fast?" asked Cat,
as Rabbit's feet slipped on papers and
sent them twisting into the air.

"Come with me,
the house is
falling down!"

Cat needed no more convincing and
padded after them. On they ran, faster
every moment, into the sitting room.

"Why are you running so fast?" demanded Dog.

His ears twitched as his toys were scattered about him by Rabbit's paws.

"Come with me, the house is falling down!"

Dog needed no more convincing and bounded
after them as they raced into the conservatory.

"Why are you running so fast?" asked
Tortoise slowly.

"Come with me, the house is falling down!"
Rabbit shrilled, knocking a delicate bloom
to the floor in his haste.

Tortoise needed no more convincing.
As petals pirouetted through the air,
he pushed himself up and tottered
after them.

On and on they hurtled, and the tortoise
tottered, until suddenly a tiny voice said . . .

Rabbit looked up at Moth with wide eyes. "But the house is falling down!" he whispered.

"Let's go and see what frightened you," said Moth kindly.

They made their way
cautiously back down the dim
corridors to the bedroom . . .

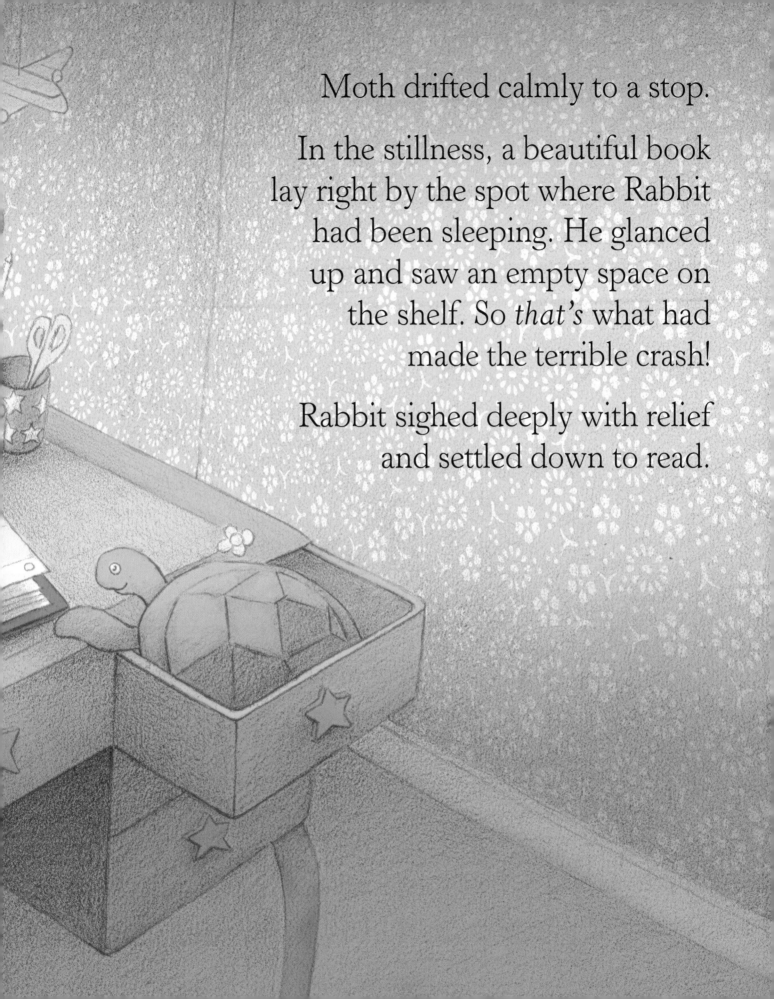

Moth drifted calmly to a stop.

In the stillness, a beautiful book lay right by the spot where Rabbit had been sleeping. He glanced up and saw an empty space on the shelf. So *that's* what had made the terrible crash!

Rabbit sighed deeply with relief and settled down to read.

In that moment, and the next,
Rabbit knew that all was well.